FLOURISHING FICTIONS

PRAISE FOR GAIL BOENNING
SHARED WITH IMMENSE GRATITUDE

The stories in this book provide an opportunity to reflect and discover who you really are... by exploring and embracing your inner dialogue. The author has identified a unique way for you to communicate with the most important person in your life, YOU!

~Bobby Kountz, author of The Someday Solution: How To Go From Unsure To Unstoppable "One Day At A Time"

I love how Gail's creative journey continues. She's not afraid to try new storytelling techniques and I find myself savoring each story, wanting to continue the conversation. Gail uses her voice as a gift to encourage us to notice the things around us and to be present in our lives.

~Ilene Levy

FLOURISHING FICTIONS

POSSIBILITIES FROM A TO Z

GAIL BOENNING

Editor: Kara Masters

Cover Art: Anya Toomre

Cover Design: Nathaniel Dasco

Photography: Gail Boenning

Chapter 19 Cardinal Photograph by Danielle Kornitz

For my Mom and Dad... who made my life possible.

The practice of contentment begins with an awareness of how we evaluate ourselves and our surroundings.
~Rolf Gates, *Meditations from the Mat*

————

Each chapter in Flourishing Fictions opens with a photo, paired with a six-word-story or haiku, written by a generous collaborator.

I was curious to find out if my family and friends would join in my game of creation. Not only am I delighted by their responses, I find that writers and poets live alongside me.

I wouldn't have been aware if I hadn't asked.

————

Six-word-story: Six words that say something powerful.

Haiku: A poem of seventeen syllables, in three lines of five, seven, and five.

INTRODUCTION

Your tricycle called LIFE arrived with round wheels. When you took it out for a spin, you pedaled over gum, rocks, and poop on the sidewalk. Your smooth ride took on bobbles and bumps.

And even though you can't see where anyone else's rubber meets the road, all us tricyclists are experiencing something similar. Or, very different? Our tires were not made on a standardized assembly line.

What if we begin again?

Start over?

Can we?

This book is about looking backward and forward while living in the present moment. Possibility and beauty hide in our thumps, wobbles, and jolts. Sometimes we've got to hop off of our three-wheelers and scrape at the tires with a stick to see what we've picked up.

Mechanics, traffic cops, your mom and dad... even a stranger in the next lane can be a helper. Relationships, like mirrors, reflect what we might otherwise miss. And yet, I've learned... the responsibility for how and where my bike travels rests ultimately with me.

The sticks I use to clean my tires are the practices of writing, sharing, and connecting. *Flourishing Fictions* rounds out a trilogy of A-Z explorations.

Wandering Words is a collection of personal essays — I started with baby steps.

Meandering Muses is a collection of dialogue-based stories, revolving around three Greek muses and me. I am known as Typist. Calliope is very curious and asks a lot of questions. Thalia overflows with a love for life. Urania keeps all of us on track as best she can.

I'm inviting the muses to start us off again here. Then we'll slip into a world of *what can be* when we ride with compassion and LOVE for ourselves and others.

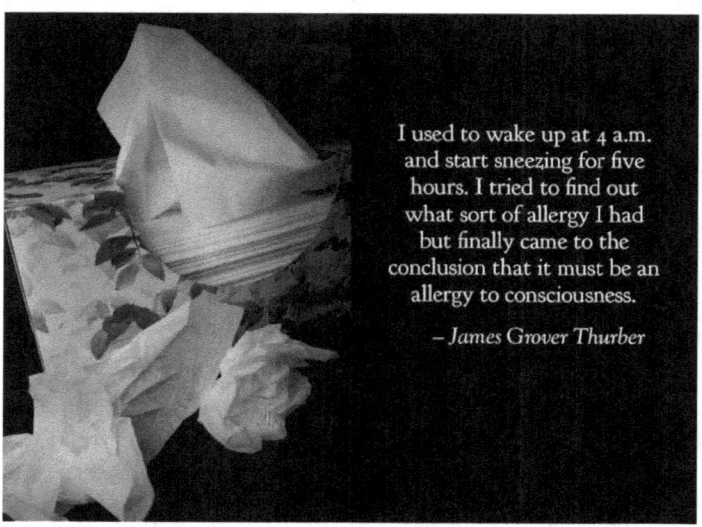

I used to wake up at 4 a.m. and start sneezing for five hours. I tried to find out what sort of allergy I had but finally came to the conclusion that it must be an allergy to consciousness.

– *James Grover Thurber*

"I don't understand," said Thalia. "How can someone be allergic to consciousness?"

"It says here..." Urania looked at Typist's phone, "... James Grover Thurber was a cartoonist."

"With a middle name like Grover, I guess a sense of humor was a necessary life skill?" Cal shrugged.

"But, I still don't get it," said Thalia.

"Perhaps he was saying it is easier to live life running the programs that we've been handed from our families and society? Instead of thinking consciously about our feelings and actions?" Cal asked.

"Hmmm... let's think about that," said Urania. "What if instead of pushing forward on autopilot... opportunities to slow down and be mindful become the *new best thing*? What are the possibilities?"

You first...

1

ABUNDANT SOLITUDE

The best book club conversation — alone.

— Julie Lopez

*N*ancy sat at the oak dining table, her back to the clock. *Tick-tick-tick* — the seconds passed, one separated from the next by a minuscule pause. The table, set with china handed down from her grandmother, was guest ready. Every plate, bowl, and cup wore a delicate flower pattern in shades of pink, green, and gold.

Lasagna baked in the oven, a salad chilled in the refrigerator, and a loaf of french bread awaited slicing. A bottle of cabernet rested uncorked, and chardonnay chilled in a silver bucket of ice. Nancy reached for the bottle of white and filled the glass in front of her.

As the clock continued to *tick-tock* behind her, Nancy congratulated herself. *Have I ever had the entire meal prepared and table set in time to catch my breath before the doorbell rang?* Usually she was still stuffing papers in drawers and shoes in closets when the first guest arrived.

The hostess took a sip from her glass, closed her eyes, and thought about her book club selection. She loved it — every single word of Steven Galloway's novel was a gift. *The Cellist of Sarajevo* grabbed Nancy from its first page and carried her through the lives of characters surviving a war they surely wanted no part in. Mental imagery painted through black typeset words ignited hope that, even in the direst circumstances, some human hearts remain true to their humanity.

Nancy picked up her glass and took another drink. *Maybe this time will be different. Maybe this time we will discuss the book.* Just maybe, instead of sitting silently *mmmm-hmmming* and *ah-haaaaaing*, Nancy would share her thoughts, even if it meant butting in and raising her voice to be heard.

Maybe.

A full-fledged people pleaser, Nancy hoped everyone liked the book. There was a lot riding on the shoulders of a hostess who not only picked the book for a ladies' night but fed everyone dinner, too.

Nancy turned to look at the clock and was surprised to

find its short arm pointing at the Roman numeral seven. *Have I been sitting lost in my own thoughts for twenty-five minutes?* She smelled her not-so-secret Italian sausage and garden vegetable lasagna baking. She got up to peek in the oven, where she found perfectly bronzed mozzarella.

Nancy turned off the oven and looked at the clock again. *Where is everyone?* She knew it was common to be a few minutes late, but almost a full half-hour past invitation time raised questions.

Nancy went to her desk and checked her calendar page. Written in pencil, it clearly said in the square for the 6th — *Book Club Hostess, 6:30, The Cellist of Sarajevo.* Hmmm. Maybe everyone was busy shuffling children or getting food on the table for their families. She'd give it a few more minutes.

Seated again, clock tick-tocking at her back, Nancy took a sip from her glass and reflected on book club gatherings — routine and predictable, seemingly comfortable affairs. Everyone arrived and was offered a drink. Guests shared in town gossip, while teasing and poking gentle fun at each other. *Was there a better way to make sure nobody escaped from the herd?* Mothers discussed their children's affairs, as if they were living through the young creatures. Occasionally, a few comments about the reading selection nudged their way into conversation. Often, a few strong voices dominated any discussion of the book and swayed general opinion to match their own.

When all invitees attended, there were just under a dozen ladies in all. Nancy found it hard to concentrate on any one conversation and often listened to more than one at a time. Like a drive-in waitress on roller skates with a full bay of sedans, she found her divided attention exhausting. Promptly at nine, she'd start looking at her watch, waiting for an opportunity to excuse herself and head home.

Ping

Nancy's phone snapped her back into the present. She looked at the text from Jen. *Where are you?*

Nancy texted back. *Where am I??? Where are you? It's almost seven and nobody is here.*

A minute or so passed and her phone pinged again. *Book club is at Rachel's tonight!*

Nancy walked to her office and checked her calendar one more time. Sure enough. She'd messed up. Her calendar was on the March page. She flipped back to February. On the sixth of February, written in pencil, it said *Book Club, Rachel's, 6:30 The Dome (King)*.

How did I mess up? She really couldn't say.

It was surely an honest mistake?

Nancy sat back down at the table, refilled her wine glass, and took a slow drink. She sent a text back to Jen. *Sorry! I guess I mixed up the date. Please go ahead without me.*

Nancy served herself lasagna with a thinly sliced piece of bread. She turned off the background music and grabbed her copy of *The Cellist of Sarajevo*. Flipping through the pages, she skimmed the highlights she'd made. She ate, making sure to leave room for an extra large serving of tiramisu.

As she enjoyed her dinner and the silence, Nancy thought, *This was the best book club ever*.

It was her last... and her first.

The best book club conversation — alone.

2

BUDDING

Unfurled and free
Letting go was meant to be
Live fully your life

– Gary Breads

$\mathcal{I}$n the beginning, I felt so tight and confined.

"It's not yet time," the icy winds roared in response to my impatience. "You must wait until the conditions are right, or you will perish before you've begun. *Have patience* — the joy of existence awaits, if only you follow the flow."

And so, curled tightly, I gathered my excitement and waited for the glorious call. When the sun's ever strengthening rays beckoned to my cells, I burst forth into leafy abandon — a bud no more.

Free... I acknowledge the sun's arc through the sky as it radiates light and heat, only to disappear, leaving darkness to the waxing and waning moon.

In all, from bud to my current state of decaying debris, I counted more than four hundred glorious cycles, light to dark — then light again.

Ahh yes! After the call to unfurl, I grew from small to large, taking note of my fellow travelers in our cluster, all of us attached by a stem to our life supporting branch — one among many extensions from our patron — a solid, healthy, thick trunk, who in turn is anchored to the earth by strong, sturdy roots. All parts of the whole owe gratitude to the tiny root hairs that draw moisture and nutrients from the surrounding soil to keep us fed and watered.

To think that *my life — the mighty oak's life —* sprouted from a dropped acorn decades ago. *What a wonder I am! What a wonder we are... all parts together!*

I now wish I'd thought to share my story sooner — while I was rich and green — so vibrant and full of life. I could have covered days and details I've no longer the strength to recount. There's no time for regret. I'll instead spill forth what is fresh, bubbling unhindered like water from the nearby spring. In presence, there is little room for regret or fear...

After darkness approached, something I'd never before experienced in my full grown splendor began to overtake me. The day had been dark and gloomy with much moisture in the air. Dampness clung to every leaf, blade, and branch.

I felt a chill settle with the sun's disappearing rays and I remembered a sensation of liquid transforming into something solid — encasing me. I was reminded of a time long ago when I was still small — before I'd opened.

Once again, I wore a tight fitting jacket that offered no warmth.

I waited and wondered — *What will the sun's rise bring?*

As dawn broke, the sun rose higher and rays bounced and twinkled upon facets of frozen dew. The world's appearance was transformed. I had no idea such beauty was possible.

The approach of feet felt different in sound and vibration today. With each step, the grass — frozen like me — held for the slightest moment before giving way to the traveler. It seemed frost was reluctant to give up its hold before shattering and scattering to the dirt below.

The traveler paused. Everyone in my cluster held tight to our branch despite our weariness. I was certain her bright eyes lingered upon my rich red fall attire — bejeweled in shimmering white. She pointed something at me that flashed like a shooting star before continuing on her way.

"Stay," I whispered with a voice she could not hear.

At the pace of a summer slug, the sun crested the tree line and leaned more intensely upon my surface. My frozen coat tickled as it melted.

Heavy — I felt so heavy. With a sigh, I let go of my branch and fell to join others who'd gone before. We littered the ground in shades of burnt umber, hazel, and garnet.

I'd like to believe that when the visitor paused on her return trip, she noticed that I'd fallen.

She did not stop, but I hope as a fellow traveler through

this world, she recognized my transience and honored my cycles and seasons. *How many trips around the sun will she enjoy?*

From my resting place, I wished her well and murmured, "Continue your adventures. Smile at the sun, the moon, and all that transpires. Cycles bleed one into the next — welcome each. One day you too will fall, but do not fear. Letting go is meant to be.

Unfurled and free
Letting go was meant to be
Live fully your life

3

CHARMED CALLIE

STRONG COCKY GAL'S HAND
POOL BREAKS COLOGNE AND PERFUME
SERENDIPITY

-- TIM JORDAN

*C*allie was fifteen minutes early. Resting her arms on varnished oak marred with sweaty-glass rings, she nodded at the bartender who sauntered over. "What can I get you?" he asked, while drying a thick mug with a flour sack dish towel.

"Pilsner — tap, please."

"24 or 36 ounces?"

"Let's go with the 36," Callie replied. "I've got three games ahead of me. I'll probably need another before I start game two. I can't believe I agreed to sub. My aim is terrible. Maybe the beer will help?"

"You know where to find me," the bartender replied. When he winked, the corners of his mouth climbed toward his cheekbones. His right cheek had a dimple to die for.

Callie passed through the alley between two pool tables and approached a group of ladies surrounding a pub table littered with rectangular slips of paper and eraserless mini pencils. They reminded her of summer days in a golf cart. Come to think of it... beer never helped her golf game.

"What's going on?" she asked a twenty-something sporting a crew cut, plaid shirt, and faded jeans.

"Radio station is running a contest. Whoever can hold a full stein the longest wins a set of darts and a logo hat. Here's the cool thing — if you win — you move on to another round. And, if you win there, you get airfare and all-inclusive lodging to, ummm... not Puerto Vallarta, hmmm... Punta Cana. That's it! Punta Cana, Mexico. Five days, four nights — for two!"

Callie grabbed a slip of paper and a pencil. She knew it was only a matter of time before she'd be lounging on the beach.

When her name was called, Little Miss Confidence rolled her sleeves above her elbows and stepped up to the line. She squeezed her triceps before giving her hands a shake to throw off any bad energy.

Callie glanced at the clock — six minutes, thirteen seconds, and counting. She and a petite pixie with pink lips and chestnut hair stood facing each other, a mere two feet between them.

"How much do those steins weigh?" someone in the crowd asked the radio deejay.

"Depends how long you hold it," the deejay replied. "If you pick it up for a sip and set it right back down... probably doesn't feel like much. To these ladies who've been at it for over seven minutes, I dunno. Ladies — how heavy is it? Like holding a piano? Get it — Stein — way?"

The crowd groaned. Pixie set her mug on the table and rubbed her wrist.

Callie *knew* that sombrero key chain in her pocket was good luck. She lifted her mug, winked at the cute bartender, and took a swig before setting her stein down. She'd won herself a ticket to the big show. Maybe the bartender would come with her to Mexico?

Strong cocky gal's hand
Pool breaks cologne and perfume
Serendipity

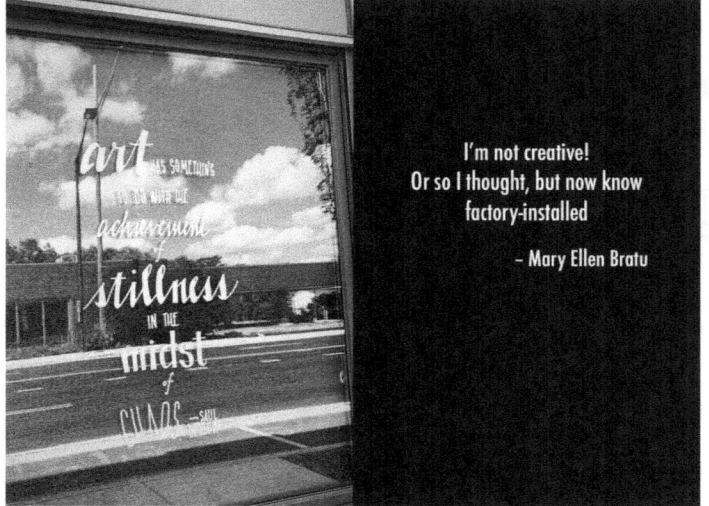

I'm not creative!
Or so I thought, but now know
factory-installed

– Mary Ellen Bratu

"*Y*ou're done waiting," I whispered to my reflection.

"*Finished* waiting?" I asked the vision of me who did not waver on the glass. From a time and place far away, my high school literature teacher's voice boomed,

"Potatoes are *done*, Miss Brush. People are finished. Now poke the spud with a fork and let's move on."

"Finished waiting!" I silently screamed at my unblinking reflection.

How many times had I walked past the studio and noticed the evenly spaced desk lights, brush sets, watercolor palettes, and lusciously over-sized canvases at each work-space? How many times had I heard piano music and his soothing voice wafting out through the open door? What was it the man in moccasins and a pull-over sweater often said? A quote from Michelangelo, was it? "The greater danger for most of us lies not in setting our aim too high and falling short, but in setting our aim too low and achieving our mark." Yes... That was it.

A harried mother, dragging two squirmy toddlers, climbed the stairs into the studio's neighboring pizza parlor. I did my best to ignore them, holding my gaze in the plate glass. *Remember when that was you?* my reflection asked. *Such a wonderful time — bustling, tending, soothing. The children needed you and you gave your all. Now it is time to care for yourself.*

"And when you are well within, you will bring your best self to every encounter, experience, and escapade. Now please use the dropper from your jar to place one drop of water on each color of your palette," instructed the man in wire-rimmed glasses.

Something about the place called to me and yet, over the course of a decade, I always found a reason to shush it into submission... until tonight... when I decided to choose myself. Earlier in the day, I'd heard a woman on the radio talking about negative waiting. She said people of all shapes, sizes, colors, and ages often carry a mistaken belief that a hero will swoop down, take their hand, and lead them to their dreams. In the meantime, they filled their hours with rushing, scrolling, and gossiping — adroitly side-stepping all the things they'd really like to try. Right before I had to turn off the car and bustle into the grocery, she asked, "Would our reality change if people learned to stop being afraid to experience life?"

"Here goes nothing... or everything. We're no longer afraid," I whispered to my reflection before stepping across the threshold into a new way of being and seeing.

Seven sets of eyes looked up from their water droppers.

"Mrs. Paint! I was beginning to think you'd never join us. How lovely that my secret wish has finally pulled you across the threshold. I've been saving a spot for you all these years." Our eyes met. There was a twinkle and a wink before the owner of The Well Within Workshop said, "Your seat is the open one at the end of the table."

I'm not creative!
Or so I thought, but now know
factory-installed

5

ELEVATED VIEW

BUS STOP GATHERINGS
OBSERVATIONS EVERYWHERE
PERSPECTIVE IS KEY

— ERICA DOHRMANN

A five-year-old with a buzz-cut tossed a wobbly pass to a second grader sporting a long auburn ponytail. Olivia wore sneakers with her pink and purple patterned sundress. She managed to catch the orange foam football and praised the little boy who lived next door for his strong arm.

"Olivia is so kind," buzz-cut's mom commented to Olivia's mom. "I appreciate how she's been keeping an eye out for Peter and making sure he gets on the right bus to come home in the afternoon."

There's nothing quite like a September morning at the bus stop. Kids are happy to have a new routine and friends to play with. Moms and dads feel relief in sharing the weight of teaching their children. Bus drivers smile and wave. Siblings in strollers gurgle and drool. Birds warble. Squirrels scamper with acorns clamped in their jaws. Chrysanthemums in shades of burnt orange, sunny yellow, and crimson smile from front porches.

And today... a plain black sedan with tinted windows drives slowly into, around, and out of the cul de sac. On the driver's door, in small white letters, are the words *Protective Services*.

"Anybody know who that is?" asked Peter's mom.

Shrugs and shakes all around.

"Ladies... We're living inside a dystopian novel," said Olivia's mom. "Big brother patrols our neighborhoods — manicured, fake-tanned, and coiffed reporters blare from our televisions — our country, divided among innumerable fault lines, is ripe for authoritarian rule." She'd meant it as a joke, but as the words floated on the cool breeze, she heard a small but persistent ring of truth.

"That was creepy," said Peter's mom. "Maybe *Protective Services* is the name of a pest control service? As the weather gets colder, mice and spiders are moving in through the cracks and crevices of our foundations."

"Maybe." Olivia's mom massaged the fingers of her right hand with the fingers from her left and looked at the ground. "Not that I know a thing about politics, newscasting, or writing screenplays... but does it seem like society is writing a script and then bringing it to life? Why do we create so many fear-inducing stories and then play them on repeat? What if we started telling more stories about what's possible, instead of what's wrong?"

As the brakes of the long yellow bus squealed, driver Ed waved from behind the wheel. Olivia let Peter climb the gigantic steps before her.

"Like Ed's story? Retired after 35 years in a foundry and he starts driving a bus because he knows there's a shortage of good drivers. He told me he's doing it because the kids are fun and it gets him out of the house. He doesn't need the money," said Peter's mom. "Gotta go... I'm taking my mother-in-law to the doctor. See you this afternoon."

"Sounds good. How about if we each bring a story of something that made us smile during our day? We can share our own stories of what's possible."

"I saw a meme in my feed this morning that said... *The maps are not the territory.* What do you think that means? And... Do you think it's interesting that we call it a *feed*?" Peter's mom asked.

"I think the saying means there are seeds of goodness and possibility just waiting for us to water them — not on the map, but ready to sprout. And yes... interesting that we call it a feed. Who is feeding us?" Olivia's mom gave Peter's mom a wave and started up the slight incline of cracked asphalt toward her open garage door. She thought of a letter she once read from E.B. White to a man who'd lost faith in humanity. He wrote something like... As long as there is one upright man or one compassionate woman, the contagion might spread and the scene is not desolate. She'd recently read *Charlotte's Web* to Olivia... White had such a way with words.

Despite a torn ACL, the family's old golden retriever Addie stood on three legs at the front door. Her tail wagged. Love and light beamed from her eyes.

What if the only thing wrong with the world is the way we choose to see it?

Bus stop gatherings
Observations everywhere
Perspective is key

6

FARSIGHTED

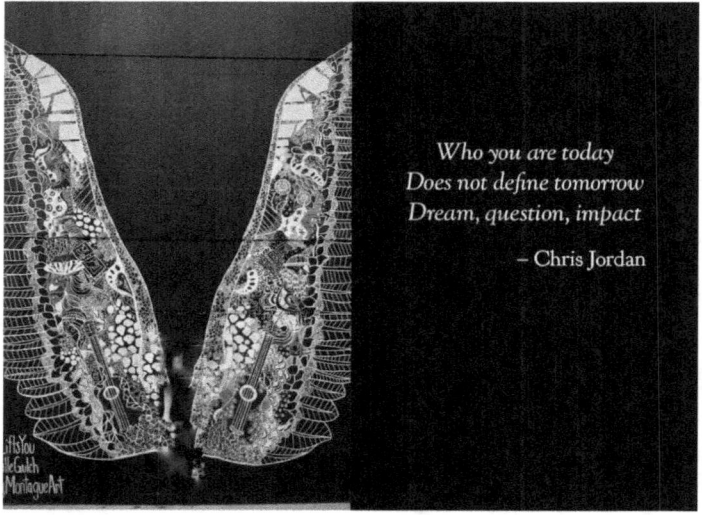

Who you are today
Does not define tomorrow
Dream, question, impact

– Chris Jordan

s a sixth grader at Darlington elementary, Jack Frank figured he knew a lot. He was a big fish in a school of guppies. On a warm May afternoon, he gazed out beyond the science room's dinosaur skeleton posters and cinder block walls onto the playground. Soon he'd be free of baby-sized desks and primary colored playground slides, swings, and monkey-bars. He could see the middle school that awaited his arrival across sandy baseball diamonds and weedy grass soccer fields.

His science teacher Mr. Lium was standing in front of the classroom's whiteboard, telling a story about the power in a butterfly's wings. A scientist once said their simple flap could affect weather patterns on the other side of earth. His fellow scientists scoffed at the suggestion until, a few decades later, some physicists proved it was true.

Blah, blah, blah... is what Jack heard until Mr. Lium said something about a guy named Norman something or other. Norman was from Iowa, just like Jack's grandparents. And... Norman worked to produce high-yield crops that fed people who might otherwise starve.

This information by itself might have skipped through Jack's brain like a flat stone on calm water but, like a dolphin, a memory leaped into the air and connected Jack with Mr. Lium's story. Last night at dinner, Jack's mother had been fretting about the news and its never-ending coverage of the pandemic. Jack's dad said, "There are too many damn people on this planet already. God's way of thinning the herd. We keep figuring out how to keep people alive and the earth's resources keep dwindling."

Jack struggled with the contradiction. *Is keeping more people alive good or bad? Was this guy Norman a good guy? Or, a bad guy? And, why was it okay for his father to swear when he got scolded for using those same words?*

Mr. Lium dropped his cowbell on the floor. He'd learned as a young teacher that noise got attention. The questions Jack had been squeezing and shaping floated out the window to join a sky full of puffy cumulus clouds. Jack's attention shifted to Mr. Lium's wrap up of the day's lesson.

"So, you see, humans create and observe, create and observe... That's the way of evolution. Sometimes — quite often — we have to create our way out of snafus we've generated, like the paper toweling commercial once said, 'Life's messy — clean it up.' To the best of my awareness, there has never been a human capable of fully understanding the mysteries of how our world works. And, it's never quite clear whether we are seeing the world as it is, or as we interpret it. Quite a beautiful conundrum."

Jack raised his hand.

"Yes Mr. Frank... What is it?"

Jack took a deep breath. "Are you saying... Well, did you just say... that it's okay to not know all of the answers?"

"Yes Jack, you heard me correctly. I hope your classmates were listening as closely as you."

Who you are today
Does not define tomorrow
Dream, question, impact

7

GUARDIAN

The sacrifice that
Precedes triumph, too often
The story untold

– Harper Thorpe

I'm not just another pretty plant, you know. I happen to play an integral role in the life cycle of the majestic monarch butterfly. Without me, the fluttering orange wings of *Danaus plexippus* would become just another marvel that *used to* be — *back when.*

I cannot speak or write like humans, but I do have stories to tell. I've observed and experienced the turning of the world, while whispering tales to the winds.

Like tufted seeds from my pods in autumn, I release stories that float and anchor. Some find purchase in fertile ground and root themselves in the minds of storytellers, where they grow ripe and rich.

Botanists call me *Asclepias syriaca* and classify me as a member of the plant kingdom. To the unscientific, I am simply known as milkweed. Today, you can call me a memory, begging to be released.

Four of her six legs touched down, resting ever so lightly upon one of my leaves. She at first chose a spot near my flowering hat, but then decided a leaf farther down would better shelter her offspring. She deposited one egg on the leaf's underside, the egg's color matching the color of the milk hidden inside my leaves. With her work complete, Faith — I call all those who flutter by that name — floated away without a backward glance.

A woman and boy who'd passed by, poking and prodding me and my neighbors over the last several days, talked excitedly when they found the cream-colored, hidden package. The woman disappeared into the large unnatural structure that blocked my morning sun. She returned with a thin, long, silver stick. She handed it to the boy, touched my stem about a third of the way down and said, "Here."

It happened so fast, I hardly knew what hit me — I'd been severed!

A good chunk of me was now housed in a glass jar with a blue top. I guessed that the egg had been captured for observation. Were those *sailboats* painted on the side of my cramped new home? Without consulting me, or the egg, the boy carried us into the structure.

At first I missed the sun, wind, and rain. I chose to focus my attention on the egg. When I felt the first subtle tug on my leaf, I knew seven cycles of light and dark had passed. Free from its shell, a tiny caterpillar tentatively began to nibble on the very leaf that sheltered it during its incubation. The little creature was ever so small, pale green, and almost translucent. Its appetite was voracious and its growth rapid.

I took note that there were no feathered fliers inside the structure, and found myself glad for the unsolicited sacrifice I'd made. I felt that offering my service as breakfast, lunch, and dinner for the yellow, white, and black-striped larvae was my role. And without predators lurking about... the possibility for a spun chrysalis making way for emergent wings had just increased exponentially.

The creeper ate and grew, ate and grew, ate and grew.

One morning when the eyes of *twolegs* peered through the glass, they were delighted to find you'd hidden yourself in a golden-edged, leaf-green cocoon. As time passed, there were moments when our world would spin as our temporary home was picked up, turned, and searched for signs of change.

"Is it still alive, Mommy? I don't see it," the boy sometimes wailed.

"Oh, child," I thought, "It's alive and well. I can feel the vibrations of miraculous transformation."

Despite my wilted condition, I felt immense joy the night of your grand emergence. How spectacular and delicate your thin black legs felt on my stem! Faith looked just like her mother.

When the sun rose, familiar eyes peered past the sailboats.

The woman said to the boy, "The breezes are calling.

We've been blessed to observe a miracle. Let's set our friend free."

Together the pair carried our jar outside. The woman reached in and you bravely stepped onto her hand. She placed you on a purple flower with great care. While you levered your wings up and down, I whispered, "Good-bye and fare-the-well, Faith."

Moments later, I was shaken from the jar to the ground. Knowing my story had been left in good hands, I released it and calmly took my rest.

The sacrifice that
Precedes triumph, too often,
The story untold

———

8

HALF TO FULL

TAKING RISKS WILL
KINDLE YOUR FIRE.

– JEANNE OLEN

*M*onica cinched her girdle of politeness so tight that she was almost invisible. Whenever she went out with friends, she declined to weigh in on any appetizer selections. "Whatever you all want is fine with me," she'd say and then end up with an empty tapas plate

when the calamari and coconut shrimp was passed around...
as if nobody knew she didn't eat seafood. Oh well, as long as
everyone else was happy, invisibility was fine for her.

Do you know what's sad though?

Monica's friends *weren't* happy. They complained that
the calamari was stringy, or the strawberry piña colada
sauce was too sweet, or the air-conditioned restaurant was
too cold. Rarely did anybody comment on how great it was
to sit down in a festive atmosphere, to be waited on, or to
have enough money for appetizers and dessert.

Monica often wished she'd just stayed home with a book
or movie. She'd read somewhere that the human brain was
still evolving and that entrenched habits of seeing the glass
half-empty would slowly fade as people woke up to their gift
of consciousness. Monica hoped the claustrophobic nega-
tivity she often felt would dissolve sooner rather than later.

When her childhood friend Tina texted to invite her to a
yoga class, Monica was intrigued. She'd been stretching
along with an Asian man on a Hawaiian beach via DVD for
well over a year. Tina's message said that the Mindful Movement yoga studio was just a few miles down the road from
her house, in a strip mall next to the garden center. Perhaps
an in-person class would offer something new? Monica's
DVDs had grown stale as a bowl of chips on a picnic table in
humid August. And so, on a frigid January morning, Monica
pulled at a locked studio door. Her car was alone in an icy
asphalt lot of spaces marked with yellow paint. She checked
her watch... only ten minutes early... *Where was everyone?*

Back in her car, Monica pulled her phone from her
purse to check for messages. Just then, Tina pulled her
black sedan into the neighboring space. When Monica
looked up, her eyes were drawn to a woman in flowing
colorful pants and a matching tank top unlocking the studio

door from the inside. Monica grabbed her rolled mat and began again. She had no awareness that she had just felled the first in a long line of dominoes.

What was Tina wearing? Tight leggings and a tank top under her unzipped, form-hugging jacket. Jane, one of the mom's from three-year-old Jake's preschool class, popped out of Tina's passenger door in tie dye lycra. Wearing thick baggy athletic pants and a hooded cotton sweatshirt, Monica felt like a tugboat surrounded by race cars on a *Which one of these doesn't belong?* worksheet.

If Monica wanted her world to look different, she was the one who'd have to loosen her grip. Just yesterday, she cracked open a fortune cookie that she'd found behind a tower of beans in the pantry. It read: *You can't go back and change the beginning, but you can start where you are and change the ending.*

Monica entered through the lotus-clad glass door and removed her sneakers on the entryway carpet. She was ready to align, strengthen, and stretch.

Did she just hear the clink of another domino?

Taking risks will kindle your fire.

9

INSPIRED

GOAL SETTING AIM HIGH
SOARING UPWARD ALMOST THERE
THE WILD BLUE YONDER

– CHRISTIANE WOOD

*M*ax grabbed the swing's metal link chains. They were cold, and he was undeterred. A playground lightweight, he had to use all his strength to pull himself onto the black-rubber, horseshoe-shaped seat. Max longed for the weightlessness of rising toward the sky and gliding back down again. Running, jumping, and swinging offered freedom from pencils, letters, and numbers.

Of course, Max couldn't explain what he felt with adult words and ideas. He was only five. With the vocabulary and experiences he had gathered in his short life, he simply thought — *I want to fly!*

On this, his third day of kindergarten, Max already decided recess was the best part of the day.

Once in the seat, Max knew what he was supposed to do to get moving. Grandma has a tree-swing in her backyard. Grandma, Mom, and Dad coach him. "Legs forward. Legs back. Legs forward. Legs back."

Mom sometimes said, "Stretch your toes to the sky and then swing your heels to your butt."

Mom was silly. When she said butt, it always made him giggle.

The problem was, Max had not really figured out how to get himself moving. Sure, he'd move a few inches forward and back, but not anywhere close to flying. To fly, Max needed a push. Once he got started and had some momentum, he could keep flying, with legs forward, legs back.

Max sat on the swing. He thrust his toes forward. He pulled his heels back. Again and again. His swing turned to the left and right.

Max was not a quitter. He took a break, let the swing straighten, and started again — sky, butt — sky, butt.

Mrs. Sherman was watching from the monkey bars. It was tough for her not to rush in to save the day. *Let them struggle a little... that's how we learn.*

After about three minutes of watching Max give his best effort, she decided it was time. Mrs. S. walked across the fresh wood chips and said, "Hey Max! I've got some extra energy in my arms. See? They're all wiggly." She shook her hands and twirled her arms in big circles. "Can I give them something to do? Can I use them to give you a push?"

"Yes, please!" Max flashed his one-tooth-missing smile. "I keep trying, but I just can't fly on my own."

And so it began... Mrs. Sherman took hold of the chains. She pushed forward and said, "One." Still holding the chains, she pulled Max backwards and then pushed forward again. "Two." On the third push, she asked, "Ready?"

Through laughter, Max yelled, "Yes!"

Mrs. Sherman pushed Max high enough that she could duck under his legs. She let go of the chains and joined the other teachers by the slide.

Max swung until the bell rang.

Wouldn't you know? By the third week of school, Max was flying all by himself.

Goal setting aim high
Soaring upward almost there
The wild blue yonder

10

JUMPING-OFF PLACE

A hole new world
of possibilities.

– Manu Satsangi

The hole where the couch once stood is more than a patch of gray plush carpet. Newly emptied, the space holds life — present, past, and future.

At this very moment... seam-split, smoke-colored, corduroy cushions are forging ahead to a land of mystery and intrigue — an apartment where a fledgling adult will explore life well beyond the walls of her childhood home. Though the connection between girl and seat remains, new adventures await.

Who knows what bodies... thighs, heels, backs, and heads will appear in the sofa's new life? Housemates might spill, plop, and sprawl without a second thought. Given away for nothing, there's no skin in the game.

No matter.

This sofa is up to the challenge of its new life, which is certain to be more interesting than a trash heap.

Will the four-seater ever feel the pull and scrape of a vacuum again?

In days gone by... the hole where the couch once stood held loungers traveling the globe via words and stories on the pages of books and magazines. Football fans munched chips, mini-meatballs, and all varieties of dips while the television broadcast tales of travail and triumph on turf. Cats and dogs sprawled, shed, and snored. The sofa's new owner, now grown and flown, once opened her gifts from Santa... and suffered through countless fevers and stomach bugs right there, in the hole where the couch once stood.

And now the whole house waits for what's possible.

Options, please?

The obvious and easy choice is to purchase and insert a new sofa, similar in style and color to the one that filled the hole before. Plug and play.

Or... What if the replacement couch introduces a new color and style, inviting the entire room to step into a new way of being?

Or... What if, instead of plastering the hole and brushing the room with a new coat of decor, something bigger is afoot?

What if this hole, inside a great room, inside a great house, is calling for new bodies... thighs, heels, backs, heads, and fresh thoughts to fill its hollows and empty spaces?

Possibilities abound.

The empty patch of plush-gray carpet whispered to anyone who might listen... *Not making a decision is a decision. Pause. Relax into this welcoming space. What if you allow, rather than force, the next step?*

A hole new world of possibilities.

11

KEYING BOUNDARIES

A captain's spy glass
Pointing our attention matters
Captains do like cats

– Robert Boyle

*a*n image of the scrawny little bird, she once was, fluttered into Linda's mind's eye. Standing alone against the gymnasium's brick wall, the plain, drab wren with a shag haircut kept her eyes downcast. Her pure white gym shoe squeaked and squawked against the polished court as she twitched the toe of her left foot.

"Okay... I guess you're on our team," the captain called. For a seventh grader, Kirk's body was ahead of its time. His deep voice echoed around the basketball hoop and pulled Linda to a middle position between her classmates. Her placement along the rope had nothing to do with her strength, skill, or enthusiasm. She was tossed where the others felt she'd do the least damage at tug-of-war.

What might not have been written on her face or posture was written in the stars. Linda was full of potential, pluck, and persistence. One day, she'd choose her own team... and win!

A vibration called Linda back from her daydream. Like a family dog hearing the jingle of its leash, Linda responded to the pull of her cell phone for what might have been the 44th time that morning. She scrolled through one social media feed after another and felt hollow, until a notification popped up on a job board she'd been watching. Like her kitten with a catnip spiked mouse, she tapped and swiped. Her sigh was long and audible.

Morton the tabby opened his eyes. Cocking his head to the left, he gave Linda eye-to-eye contact, his feline way of telling her that he was listening.

"Nope... Nothing to see here Mort, just another creep looking to find female companionship through a screen."

Linda prickled at her use of the word creep. *How do I know?* And so, she did what she always does — sent a quick response. She was nothing if not polite. She couldn't see the harm in using her manners... except to her own soul.

After a few back and forths, Linda learned Rainy worked on an oil rig and was a widower with a child in boarding school. She'd heard a similar story two times this week from other rig men and wondered if a copy of her profile picture was circulating in the rig's cafeteria. *Do rigs have cafeterias? Sleeping rooms with bunk beds?* She made a mental note to look up oil rig living conditions.

"Perhaps I should just delete my account? I rarely get anyone contacting me about jobs." Mort was back to snuffling in his sleep, but Linda continued to talk out loud. "Remember the story about the guy who was being scammed online for money by a kid in Nigeria? Instead of getting angry, he challenged the kid by sending him not money but a camera. He asked him to send pictures from his life and community and said he'd pay for the pictures if they were any good. If I remember correctly, the two actually built a relationship and went on to write a book together. Amazing what can happen when one human makes the time to really see another, right?"

Mort stretched on his pillow and began grooming his whiskers. His rough pink tongue rasped against his paw. Linda stuffed her phone under the couch cushion and went to do the dishes.

Several days of wake, work, and sleep cycled. Linda kept responding to Rainy — polite, but Cautious with a capital C. The virtual stranger's messages increased and Linda didn't like the needy expectation she was sensing from this man she'd never met.

"How can I set and hold a boundary while still being polite and honest?" Linda asked Morton. The cat batted a baby blue plastic ball across the foyer's tile and gave chase. Linda laughed. "Humor! Thanks — You big goof!"

She picked up her phone and typed a message...

Hi Rainy!

I thought about you in the middle of the night. Now before you get excited... Let me tell you why.

First, when I stopped responding to your messages — I felt uncomfortable for being rude.

Second, the stories you have shared about yourself tell me you have much to be grateful for. I am happy to know your daughter is blessed with a caring father.

Third, despite this, I cannot continue this conversation. I have a full life with engaging work, good friends, and a demanding cat who always has my back.

Wishing you the best!

L

Boundary set... Linda gave Morton a scratch, slipped on her sneakers, and headed out for a jog under a clear blue sky. She'd found a way to tug for her team by saying "No, thank you," while being kind to Rainy... and a tad funny. Win win.

"Morton?" Linda scratched her cat's forehead. "Stronger and clearer every day. Let's keep growing."

A captain's spyglass
Pointing our attention matters
Captains do like cats

12

LONGING

One gray morning and
A hot cup of coffee with
Thoughts of future love

– Ari Lopez

*A*s she walked past the dress shop window, single Scarlet gazed longingly at swaths and poofs of white fabric. Satins and tulles draped and flowed, accented with beads. Oh, how she yearned to share her morning coffee and bagel with a special someone sitting across from her at their dinette table.

She'd say, "Can you pass me the butter please?"

And, since he was getting up to let their mewling Zoe in the back door anyhow, he'd reply, "Of course, dear. Can I warm up your coffee?" With the subtlety of a lion, Zoe had just given the door a scratch and bolstered the racket with meows that begged, "Let me in — and will you fill my saucer while you're at it?"

No-longer-single Scarlet's ever attentive husband would fill her cup with rich, robust, steaming black coffee from the percolator and top it off with cream from a little cow-shaped pitcher. He'd bellow, "Moooooooo," as he poured a bit into Zoe's saucer.

Scarlet just loved him, this imaginary man.

Shaking her head free of the dream, the window gazer scolded herself. "This needs to stop! If a husband, home — *Gasp! Dare I wish for so much?* — and family find me, it will not be because I have frittered away months searching for them."

What was that thing her father used to say? All good things come to those who wait? Serve no wine before its time? Do what's expected and, when least expected, untold rewards will come?

Ugh! It didn't matter.

What did matter was the mountain of put off work, professional and personal, that continued to mount as Scarlet kept her nose to the ground, sniffing for Mr. Right. Although neat and tidy, the stacks of files on her desk were growing above the height of her coffee cup. She tried to concentrate... She really tried! But, one minute she would be looking at facts and figures and then the next, almost as if her hands moved without any conscious thought, she'd be scrolling through an article with a title like: *180 Ways to Find the Right Man* or *How to be a Man Magnet*. Sometimes, half an hour or more would pass before she caught herself. She'd muscle her mind back to balance sheets, but within minutes, she'd find herself scrolling through photos of wedding bouquets.

At home, Scarlet's sink was full of dishes. Laundry burst out of the chute and cascaded onto the floor. Her refrigerator held only a squeeze bottle of ketchup, pre-cut carrots, and expired yogurt. Dust bunnies played tag every time she walked down the hallway.

The worst part was not that her work and home had become secondary to runaway thoughts jogging through her mind... No, the worst part was that she could not break the cycle of obsession, despite a nagging recognition of how bad it was for her. And, even though she suspected shaming herself wasn't helping, she shamed herself anyway.

For a few days now, Scarlet had been imitating a movie scene she once watched. A man with gray stubble got up in the morning, peered at his hazy reflection in his cracked bathroom mirror and said, "Thank you, God, for letting me have another day."

Scarlet was doing her best to create new habits. And still... she hopped from one guilt mountaintop to another. She felt alone. Every time she brought up the subject of her obsession with her family or friends, they made light of it, or offered ridiculous advice: "Have you tried signing up for the singles group at church?" or "Single is the new mauve." Utterly useless.

Her obsession felt like a never-ending, dull toothache. She was beginning to wonder if she'd have to seek professional help. A little voice from inside whispered, "You need a distraction that is big and exciting enough to take your mind off of finding a husband — more presence, less searching."

On a drizzly gray morning, Scarlet drove to the animal shelter. She'd signed up to volunteer as a dog walker and cat playmate. There's nothing quite like playful, warm, energetic bundles-of-love to invite attention.

When she stopped to sign in at the welcome desk, Logan greeted her with a warm handshake and a smile. "Let me show you around," he said. "Can I get you a cup of coffee? If you take cream, there's half & half in the little cow-shaped pitcher on the refrigerator's top shelf."

One gray morning and
A hot cup of coffee with
Thoughts of future love

13

MINING CURIOSITY

Freedom can be a
complicated
concept.

– GJ Boenning

*S*o many want to simplify. They want an easy answer to this problem or that issue. Minds see right or wrong — black or white.

Reality is full of every shade in between.

People form opinions — choose a side. Hearsay and

gossip sway their minds to follow without question and to neglect independent thought. Those, who have yet to understand everything is connected, call mindlessly for your destruction. They've heard about that chihuahua or tabby you took for your lunch.

Your supporters demand your protection despite haunting nighttime howls, rabbit fur scat, and overturned trash cans.

Like your thick winter coat, there is a great gray palette beyond the blackest black and whitest white.

A flash of movement caught my eye as I jogged up the hill. You saw me, too. First you paused, then gracefully loped a hundred feet or more before freezing, eyes trained on my own halted form. We sized each other up. I had no fear and focused on your beauty. I raised a hand and called a soft *hello*. If you were afraid, you hid it well, not a muscle moved while we held each other's gaze.

I needed to keep moving; a cold wind was chilling my sweat. *Bye,* I whispered and ran on, hoping we might cross paths again in the next cul de sac. We didn't, but your image stayed with me.

Many years ago I was working at our kitchen island when my youngest daughter said, "Mommy, Ellie is playing with another dog."

Surrounded by six natural acres, we never had visits from neighbor's dogs. "Sure kid," I said, chalking it up to her imagination. I dried my hands and walked to the bank of windows overlooking our backyard. *What did I see?* Our 95 pound black lab was snout to snout with a rail thin coyote. I immediately opened the sliding glass door and stepped onto the deck.

"Ellie!" I called.

At the sound of my voice, the coyote ran into the underbrush and Ellie came trotting up the hill. Once on the deck, she nuzzled my hand, expecting a treat.

This dance of humans and nature does not have any clear answers.

I haven't read books on wildlife biology or coyote behavior.

Have you?

And... I don't fully understand the ramifications of human sprawl combined with coyote population growth. I certainly cannot foresee the future. I'm not a city planner or expert naturalist, but a quick internet search let me know that experts are studying human/coyote interactions in suburban areas. I once read an article that offered curiosity as an antidote to pangs of uncertainty. I remember the piece said something like...

Coyotes are adaptable, intelligent, and resilient animals. They have learned how to survive within a changing environment. Our challenge is to figure out how to coexist with them.

I can see the beauty of a coyote on a crisp, sunny morning and also feel the hurt of a family whose pet disappeared into the jaws of a hungry wild animal.

There's no clear right or wrong here — just many shades of trying to do what's in the best interest of all.

How could this be accomplished?

With open minds and curiosity — a willingness to learn and experiment.

Freedom can be a complicated concept.

14

NIMBLE

Lace, diamonds, and pearls
Something borrowed, blue, and new
A dress waits for you

– Erin Flores

*P*aige's frustration at trying to thread a frayed end through a tiny needle was written all over her slumped posture. Her body sat on the floor of her grandmother's sewing room while her mind drifted out the window and across town to the career counseling class she'd attended that morning.

"Gran? How'd you know you wanted to sew dresses?"

"Well... Let me think for a minute Paige. That's quite a question." Gran turned away from an intricate bead pattern she'd been working on for days. What kept her going was a vision of the bride's beaming smile. "Are you feeling troubled by a world pushing you to choose what you'll be when you grow up? There's quite a lot of pressure on the shoulders of the young these days."

Paige poked her needle into a red apple pin cushion and uncrossed her legs.

Gran continued, "I suppose it was my interest in fabrics and hemlines... models, billboards, and fashion magazines. Your great grandpa threatened to call the magazine companies to cut off my subscriptions when I failed biology."

Paige smiled at the woman whose eyes she shared. When Gran smiled back, the pair's matching dimples danced across the room. "How many weddings have you been invited to? Seems like you and Granddad are dressing up and stepping out every weekend."

Gran sighed and gazed through the window at the tall, strong maple's yellow and orange leaves. Autumn and spring were her favorite seasons. She experienced the transitions as nature's gift — a yearly reminder that all living things cycle. True joy, she thought, was found in accepting impermanence. She'd once cut out a verse from an old Bible she picked up at a rummage sale. To this day, the poem hangs on the fridge secured by a magnet that reads *Friends are the family we choose for ourselves.*

> *To every thing there is a season,*
> *and a time to every purpose under the heaven:*
> *A time to be born, a time to die;*

> *a time to plant, and a time to pluck up that which*
> *is planted;*
> *A time to kill, and a time to heal;*
> *a time to break down, and a time to build up;*
> *A time to weep, and a time to laugh;*
> *a time to mourn, and a time to dance;*
> *A time to cast away stones, and a time to gather*
> *stones together;*
> *a time to embrace, and a time to refrain from*
> *embracing;*
> *A time to get, and a time to lose;*
> *a time to keep, and a time to cast away;*
> *A time to rend, and a time to sew;*
> *a time to keep silence, and a time to speak;*
> *A time to love, and a time to hate;*
> *A time of war, and a time of peace.*
> *Ecclesiastes 3: 1-8*

"Gran?" Apparently, Paige wasn't the only one whose mind wandered away from her body. She wasn't sure what to think about that.

"Sorry Paige... Got lost in my thoughts. How many weddings? I'm not really sure. Most of the couples I've sewn dresses for have invited us to join in their celebrations. We usually go if they're local... and if I like them." Gran giggled. "Some brides can be real pains in the pincushion, if you know what I mean. I try to let a lot slide because they're young and wrapped up in all of their thoughts of what they think a wedding should be. I'd like to believe I've helped to settle some nerves while sharing some life experience along the way."

"Of all the dresses you've sewn, do you have a favorite?"

"Of course I do. It was a satin christening gown. You

wore it, as did your sister, brothers, and cousins. By the grace of God, all spit-ups and leaky diaper messes have washed out." Gran pointed to a zippered bag hanging in the closet. "Ready for action, if and when great-grandkids start appearing."

Gran took a seat next to Paige on the floor and started braiding her long hair as she'd done since the child was three or four.

"Paige, I think there's a seed inside each of us. If we give it our attention, feed and water it, follow what that little voice inside whispers when we're quiet enough to hear it... Life is beautiful. Don't worry so much about what your career is going to be. Focus instead on the kind of person Paige wants to be and the rest will sort itself out."

"Gran... I didn't like the personality test results I received today. They said I should be an accountant, or a tax lawyer, or a bookkeeper. That all sounds so dull."

"You're not tied to any piece of paper spit out by a computer, Paige... Or, advice doled out by any authority figures. Never shrink yourself for someone else's comfort."

Paige sprang up from the floor and gave Gran a great big hug. "Thanks! I gotta get going. I didn't realize the time. I signed up for a graphic design class at the library and it starts in fifteen minutes."

Left alone in her sewing room, surrounded by beads, white thread, and tulle, Gran had little doubt that Paige was going to make the most of the life she'd been given.

Lace, diamonds, and pearls
Something borrowed, blue, and new
A dress waits for you

———————

15

OUTBREATH

Eric recalls trick
While Evie practices breath
Adventure awaits

– *Sarah Brenes*

oonlight glinted on the spaniel's roan coat. Eric had chosen the breed for its hunting prowess. Much to his dismay, the predator volume button on the pup he and Evie brought home from the breeder was set awfully high and he found himself challenged to find a way to turn it down.

Out walking the neighborhood before sunrise, leash firmly in hand, Eric was aware his awareness was inferior to Frank's. They'd named the pup after Evie's grandfather who'd departed for the great meadow beyond last spring. Evie agreed that Eric could pick out the pup so long as she could name it — Frank, if it was a boy, Frances for a girl — either way, she intended to call their first baby Frankie. As part of pre-new-addition negotiations, Eric agreed to take on the morning shift. "I'm not prancing around the neighborhood in the dark," Evie said. "I'll walk Frankie in the afternoons."

Sure enough, right in front of the Swift's drive, Frankie froze and crouched. Without his glasses, Eric couldn't see what Frank was stalking... Cat? Rabbit? Surely, it wasn't a squirrel or chipmunk because neither sat still long enough to be stalked. "Where is the rabbit, Frank?" Eric squinted and scanned the rise where a grassy ditch met his neighbor's front yard that was festooned with pink flamingos from Jane Swift's 50th birthday bash. Eric's eye caught a twitch of the cottontail's long ears. "C'mon beast — no hunting. I still need to make coffee and shower. You know that."

Frank might have been familiar with Eric's routine, but didn't give a woof. He only had eyes for the hopper. His canine instincts froze him in place so that the bunny didn't make haste for the tree line.

Eric tugged. Frank didn't budge.

Eric swore. Frank ignored him.

Eric pursed his lips and blew a huge puff of stale breath into Frank's face.

The spell was broken. Frank and Eric walked on.

Evie had discovered the trick and, when Eric had

enough wits about him to remember it, a puff of air saved him countless minutes of waiting.

"Good boy. You can have a rabbit stare down on Evie's afternoon shift, okay?"

The pair kept a brisk pace going forward. Eric welcomed a cool autumn breeze and the feel of his soft, fleece sweatshirt. He wondered what it would be like to operate on instinct like Frank. *What if I had the time and patience to observe and move on nature's time?*

Sometimes you'd catch the rabbit, and sometimes you'd miss. Eric had cultivated a habit of talking to himself. *Time and patience is a luxury you can't afford pal. You gotta move if you're gonna get ahead.*

While Eric and Frank were out walking, Evie took the opportunity for twenty uninterrupted minutes on her yoga mat. Frank loved to weave between her arms and legs while she was in puppy pose or downward dog. She giggled at the thought of dogs teaching humans yoga and appreciated that yoga was called *a practice.*

Fingertips clawing the floor, shoulders rooted into their sockets, hips raised and heels descending, Evie took in a long deep breath and then let it go like honey pouring from a jar, slow and sweet.

Evie thought about how grateful she was for the local studio and teacher she'd found several years ago. Her practice's progress was like a baby learning to walk — she accepted her falls and kept going. Evie was learning how to find balance between effort and ease on her mat and beyond. A framed photo of a lion on Evie's desk was captioned: *Being both soft and strong is a combination very few have mastered.*

Evie was determined to practice mastering the combination for the rest of her life.

Her bi-weekly classes began with five sun salutations. At the end of each salute, students paused for five breaths. *Why five?* Evie thought the teacher had explained, but she couldn't remember the reason. Perhaps the logic didn't stick because she never took five breaths. Maybe she had abnormally large lungs, or she was just a slow breather, but at her pace, Evie's five breaths would hold up the rest of the group.

There was a time in Evie's life when she would have rushed five breaths to follow the rules — to be equal. She couldn't pinpoint an exact pivot, but recognized she'd been experiencing a gradual awakening. Evie had been learning to listen closely to her internal voice — her intuition. Her trust in the voice grew stronger day by day and when it told her to take three deep, rich breaths — a compromise to serve herself and others — she listened. What Evie valued was the opportunity to participate. She defined equality on her own terms... Equality is an opportunity to know the edges and interior of my puzzle piece, to observe the systems I am a part of, to contribute accordingly, and to find balance between *freedom from* and *freedom to*.

Frankie bounded in the front door, tail wagging and nails scrabbling for purchase on the floor tiles. Snout to cheek, Evie was defenseless against her pal's enthusiasm. "How was the walk?" she asked.

"Oh, you know... the usual — squirrels, rabbits, and tug-of-war. When I can remember your trick of blowing at him, a simple puff of air keeps us moving every time. Thanks for that."

"Glad I figured it out. Even though Frank sometimes feels like a heavy sack of potatoes, he's a great inspiration. Because of him, I'm... we're... learning a lot about ourselves. Stretching our patience and awareness will come in handy for our next adventure."

"Yeah, what's that?"

"What crawls before it walks and walks before it runs?" asked Evie. "Starts with a B and ends with a Y."

And in a flash, Frankie was no longer the new kid on the block.

Eric recalls trick
While Evie practices breath
Adventure awaits

16

PINCH

Beets
$2.⁰⁰

*Let go of
arbitrary worries...
live!*

– Emmett Mulrooney

𝓛 ike a pin between his eyebrows, Jared felt the pinch of generosity. After reading a plea for assistance on a scrap of cardboard, he made eye contact with the camo-clad, bearded man who sat with his back against the brick of the hardware store's facade.

"Can you spare some change for a vet down on his luck?"

Jared silently cursed himself for looking and replied, "Let me think about it." Cued by his proximity, the sliding doors opened and Jared slid into a vestibule brimming with orange shopping and platform carts. He pulled on the handle of a trolley and set off in search of the lumber he needed to repair a leaky window.

When he'd left home, his mood was as sour as his grandmother's homemade kraut. He was chewing on frustration because he had to spend a magnificent fall Saturday making home repairs. Walking past rugs, unconnected toilets, and furnace filters, Jared wondered if he should give the beggar some cash on his way out. He never knew what the *right* answer was... the well worn cliche about giving versus teaching a man to fish swam through his mind. *What if the actual action isn't what matters? What if it's the intention behind the action? Would the dude spend the money on booze? Or, something else? Does he have a car? A bank account? Only the clothes on his back?*

Jared maneuvered his cart with 2x8s through the checkout and then the sliding glass doors. He had decided to toss a few singles into the guy's cup but found that the man had gone. Jared stuffed the cash back into his pocket, loaded the lumber into the back of his pick-up, and returned the trolley to a parking lot corral.

On the drive home, he thought about his son's disappointment when he told him they wouldn't be heading out in their kayaks today. He hated disappointing the kid. Perhaps that was the real reason for his unsavory mood. Maybe, if all went well, he could fix the window and still get out for an hour or two on the river. He was aware he could turn the course of the day as easily as the power steering on his truck. If only he could shush all of the *if onlys, shoulds*, and *why don't yous* in his head, he might be able to salvage the rest of this day. Here he was — angry — about fixing something the guy sitting on the ground maybe couldn't even imagine owning.

A few weeks later, when his family strolled the asphalt aisles of an outdoor farmers' market, Jared took an opportunity to act on his thinking. Instead of stuffing the change from the lettuce vendor back into his pocket, he tossed the singles into a busker's open guitar case. He made eye contact, smiled, and nodded. *What if life is about our intentions?*

Let go of arbitrary worries... live!

17

QUALITY

Sibling love can last
a lifetime.

— Jean Lindberg

oday at the grocery checkout, I was given a story of pure, true love. It was not the kind of tumultuous affair from the cover of a magazine, tabloid, or romance novel. Nope, I saw and heard the whole spectacle with my own eyes and ears. The love story did not cost more than my attention and nourished my soul.

As young Ben scanned my groceries, he asked the occasional question about my choices,

"Why do people buy frozen juice concentrate?" — *Because it's less expensive, takes less packaging, and I can dilute it to my preference.*

"Is this parsley?" — *Cilantro, if you squeeze and sniff it, you can tell what it is, but customers will probably not like it... if you squeeze their produce.*

"What do you use it for?" — *Guacamole — rice with black beans, lime, and cilantro. You know, like they offer at one of those build your own burrito chains.*

Ben nodded and kept scanning.

My attention divided, I managed to watch a scene play out behind me.

A blue-eyed, blonde beauty walked around a heaped grocery cart and wrapped her jean-jacketed arms around the head of a handsome blond boy. He also had blue eyes. Deep dimples softened his noticeably fresh haircut. I wished I could pinch his cheeks. The pair could have been brother and sister. Oh, wait! — they were.

The boy grabbed his sister's arms, placed them back at her sides, and said, "Not in public."

"Is this — public?" she quizzically asked her mom, who was browsing through a magazine.

"Yes," her mom replied absently.

I couldn't help myself. I laughed out loud — loud enough for mom to look up from her magazine and make eye contact. Then, she laughed, too.

"I only have one," I said. "I've always wondered what it would have been like if I'd had two."

She replied, "Sometimes it's a wild ride. They can go

from loving to hating each other within a split second. Was she trying to kiss him?"

"Maybe she was leading up to that," I said.

"He'll allow it at home, but not when we're out," she said.

My attention was drawn to Alice, who was generously bagging my groceries. "Your fabric bags are full. Would you like paper or plastic for the rest?" she asked.

"Will you use paper today, please? It's back-to-school, time-to-cover-textbook season," I said with a grin.

"No problem," she answered. "My grandkids in California don't have textbooks anymore. Everything is on the computer now."

Alice and I chatted for a minute about the speed at which the world turns these days while she put the last items into a brown paper sack for me.

I thanked her and Ben and turned to the mom behind me. She was transferring apples from her cart to the conveyor belt. Her son continued to gaze at the gum and candy flanking the register aisle. His wishful thinking was written across his features. The boy's little sister was peeking from behind the cart's red push handle.

"Excuse me," I asked. "Do you mind telling me how old they are?"

Mom smiled and said, "He's six and she's four."

"Thanks," I smiled. "I hope you guys have a fantastic day."

On my drive home, I felt nourished from the crown of my head to the tips of my toes even though I hadn't eaten a thing.

Sibling love can last a lifetime.

18

REVEAL

A heavy heart
shares my lunch.

– Gloria Rios

*D*ear friend,
  When you told us today, I tried to put myself into your shoes. Our lives are similar. Can I get them on, your shoes — your experiences?

I didn't like the way they felt — too tight. The pain — *your pain* — took my breath away.

Varied in age and experience, we shared soup and salad at a table for four amid a lunchtime rush. We carried forth connections formed twenty odd years ago in an office building where our cubicles lay scattered throughout an open floor plan like coins shaken from a piggy bank. We shared stories — lunching on microwaved leftovers and strolling the neighborhood that surrounded our cream-brick, 9-5 home.

Years passed.

We drifted apart like autumn leaves on a September breeze.

Retirement, families to raise, travel, and parents to care for took us down different paths. In the past year, we've made time to rediscover each other, tossing our experiences together much like the ingredients in the food set on the table before us. And, for as much as our lives have changed, the essence of *who we are* has held steady, even if *what we do* is different.

Today we shared a typical conversation. How are the grandkids? Your mother — ninety-three! — and she still lives alone? You're leaving for Africa on Friday... you'll bring pictures next time? Things in the office are the same, but worse? Have you heard from so-and-so? How is your garden?

The entire time, I did not know you were sitting with a dagger in your heart.

After our cheerful server cleared the dishes and delivered our checks, you said, "I didn't want to come today, but I did because I said I would. I wasn't going to say anything..." You crumpled into tears.

My heart sank as my mind raced. *Are you sick? Cancer? Has something happened in your family? Divorce?*

We did what people do.

Like in a film or dream, the friend next to you slipped her arm around your back. I reached across the table and rested my hand on your arm. What? What is it? Six eyes and three hearts whispered... *What? What is happening?*

You spoke through your tears, words interrupted by pauses and irregular intakes of breath. "He's moved out."

Empathic emotion churned in my stomach along with lettuce and gnocchi. *You have a son who just started high school. Our lives are similar. Your husband has moved out... left you.* I worked to digest my thoughts.

As I laced on your shoes, I felt the strangle. Your questions of... How? Now what? How will I go on? I tried to sort, reason, and listen all at the same time.

Each of us at the table showed care and concern as we best know how to express it.

Our office mother recalled her past experience. She'd walked a similar path many years ago — before any of us had ever met. As she offered her well intentioned advice, I suspected some of her suggestions did not suit you. I watched you nod and listen with respect through your anguish. *So you.*

The friend sitting at a diagonal could not make physical contact across the table. She rose, walked around, and hugged you from behind. *Was her practical, no-nonsense-ness overcome by her feelings? Did your expression of vulnerability draw out a piece of her I have never seen before?*

You were so brave to share... to come today... even though you didn't want to.

I know *you know* these friends will come, if you call.

True to form, I reacted by saying little. You did not know

it, but the noise in my head was deafening. I kept my hand on your arm, I suspect, more for myself than for you. I made sure to get your telephone number — a closer connection than email. Although I am the same soul you met those many years ago, I've grown over time. I've learned that when we shed layers and set our shields down, we make room for connection and support to flow in.

Wearing your shoes, whether they are slogging through mud or racing downhill like an unmanned cart with a broken wheel, I know I cannot fix this. You will not hear any advice or *you-shoulds* outta me.

Know that I am here.

I like to walk. *Do you want to go for a walk?* I like to cook. *Can I drop off a pan of lasagna?* I like quotes. *Do you like this one from Harriet Tubman?*

"Our roots are in new soil, and over time, a new life will grow up around us."

I offer friendship and love.

I see and hear you.

I just watched you take a courageous step.

I am here — to cheer — your climb.

A heavy heart shares my lunch.

19

SERVING UP HOPE

Quiet solace — joyful sound;
nature's renewal.

— Sharon Boenning

This too shall pass.
A white linen shawl of snow cloaks my tiny view of the world this morning, while Mother Nature serves hope as an accompaniment to my shivers, shakes, and dim view.

Sometimes a tease, she beacons thoughts of sun-drenched days in sundresses.

A master of incremental shifts, moonlight hours shorten in equal measure to daylight's expanse. Mother Nature has an understanding of mathematics beyond numbers and symbols. I suspect she considers the practice as playfully as a writer dances with words, or an alchemist turns iron into gold. What need has Nature for clocks, protractors, and slide rules?

The distance between sunrise and sunset stretches, like bubble gum pulled by pudgy fingers in childhood. We welcome the light. Putting the dark to bed feels liberating and spirits lighten with the shift.

This morning a sound of spring twirled — familiar and welcome — inside an icy breeze. The twitter-chirp came only once, but was clear enough to be heard over the petty complaints in my mind.

The halloo spoke of shifting possibilities from dormancy to vibrant living.

Northern Cardinals wear vivid red plumage with a crest of spiked feathers upon their heads. The birds brighten winter months in the upper Midwest. They are not fair weather friends who head south when darkness, cold, snow, and ice creep upon us. And, though their song all but silences through autumn and winter seasons, they call out in January with a reminder, fleeting as it might be, that spring is indeed making its way home.

The feathered notice before we do. Without churning chatter of what was or what might be, the fliers are present for what is.

Let us be ever grateful for their generous nudge — reminding us of brighter days ahead.

When the sun hides, we tend to forget, and find ourselves mired in a mirage of ceaseless cold and dark.

Then like magic, the great mystery of life sends friends to remind us that this too shall pass.

Quiet solace — joyful sound; nature's renewal.

20

T-SHIRTS

pruning your garden —
wardrobe mind and heart — making
space for more blossoms

– Kara Masters

*M*ichael hummed Simon and Garfunkel's "Slow down, you move too fast... You got to make the morning last," as he pulled t-shirts from his dresser. His wife had been asking him to make space for months. When she put away the week's laundry and slid his drawers back into their slots, fabric snagged on the dresser's inner frame and bulged out through the connecting joints.

One Saturday morning, when his favorite royal blue workout shirt came out of the drawer with a pulled thread and splinters embedded in the fabric, Michael paused. *Why do I feel so much resistance about letting go? Jamie made a great point about shedding the old so that I have room to grow into the new. What do I need all of these shirts for?*

Like an archeologist, Micheal removed the drawer's first layer of workout shirts and lightweight tees. Underneath the everyday habitual choices, Michael began exploring the heart of the matter. Every shirt in the drawer carried a memory. There were team logos and concert tour dates — charity 5Ks and cartoon characters. The pile of printed fabrics was a pile of feelings and memories.

Jamie climbed the stairs and stopped at the door when she saw what Michael was doing. She considered sneaking back down to the kitchen on tiptoe. She didn't want to start the weekend with a fight. Michael had made it clear he did not need her advice when it came to storing his things. Instead of disappearing, she asked, "A lot of memories, huh? How's it going?"

"Mostly good... with a dash of bad," he replied. "There's a lot here to think about... It was easier to keep stuffing and smooshing." Michael held up three different shirts from a local winery's annual grape stomp. "I'm not sure why letting go is so difficult."

"I used to feel the same... like giving up stuff was saying good-bye to pieces of myself. I'm not sure what shifted that belief inside of me, but I'm glad to be rid of it. The less I carry, the more energy I have. And when I have more energy,

I'm lighter. There's more room for possibility, experience, and joy."

Michael tossed Jamie a grin and began humming, "Hit the road Jack and don't you come back... No more, no more, no more, no more..."

pruning your garden —
wardrobe mind and heart — making
space for more blossoms

21

UNBINDING

JUST CREATE; STAY CURIOUS;
BE GRATEFUL.

-- CHRIS PALMORE

*J*eff turned his face toward the floor. He'd dropped his pen with intention. Aware that his eyes spoke as loud as his voice, he avoided eye contact and kept his lips sealed. Taking long sips of air through his nose, Jeff fiddled with his pen. His face was less than a half-foot away from the floor's cool, slate-gray tiles. The marketing manager gave himself a moment to observe a flash of embarrassment that crept red and hot from his collarbones to his hairline. He knew his frustration would fade, if he just gave it a nod of recognition and a moment or two to breathe. A natural blusher since childhood, Jeff had learned that shaming himself for his body's reaction to his feelings was folly that only served to deepen his crimson hue.

He'd wanted this job.

He'd filled out his application with the care and attention of a king's tailor, minding every measured stitch.

He'd drilled himself on every possible interview question he could dream up, playing the role of questioner and respondent.

He got the job.

Jeff loved it...

and hated it at the same time.

Life was very different inside the walls of SOBS — a place where everyone agreed to practice the not-so-subtle art of radical truth and transparency. There was only one truth withheld... Not a single co-worker could tell Jeff what SOBS stood for. And even though Jeff learned from his father that to *assume* made an ass out of u & me, he figured SOBS meant that this place could make you cry.

Friday September third was Jenny's first day as Jeff's collaborator. SOBS started all employees on a Friday so that they could absorb and process their first work day experience over a weekend. Many new employees did not return on the following Monday. After the conversation Jen just witnessed, she might be one of the many.

With an overflowing basket of enthusiasm, Jeff had just shared a video he'd been working on — a narrated, emotion-eliciting whimsy about a child who'd rescued a litter of kittens from a bumbling Saint Bernard puppy. Anchoring the story was a photo of a plump pixie with blonde pigtails. She was quite literally crawling with furry fluff balls. In the blurred background, a sad looking *saint* peered through a wire mesh kennel. Jen felt the puppy's eyes say, "I was only trying to play."

When the short film stopped playing on Jeff's monitor, without a single word of support, Annette peppered Jeff with questions. "That's... interesting. Is the story real? You want to use *that* video in our outreach campaign? Do you know the child? She and her little tribe of whelps are cute... but I'm not clear as to the point you are trying to make. Where did you get this story from? It feels familiar. Is it from the internet? Do you have permission to use the story and its photo?" Annette shrugged. The black letters spelling out *Clarity is Kindness* on her t-shirt rose and fell. That's when Jeff fumbled his pen. After righting himself in his rolling chair, he looked from Annette to Jen and then went back to fiddling with his ball point.

Jeff cleared his throat. "Thanks for watching Annette — and for your questions."

"No problem. I've got to get back to my desk."

Jen twisted a blouse button at her wrist, avoiding eye contact. *What just happened?* Witnessing her new friend shift from excitement about his work-in-progress to embarrassment made Jen's stomach feel like that time in fourth grade when she rode her first roller coaster. *Interesting how Jeff offered gratitude for what I find bewildering.* Instead of riding a wave of misunderstanding, she asked, "How do you feel about Annette's questions? And what is a whelp? A kitten?"

"Welcome to your first day of disorien... I mean orientation." Jeff smiled. "Initially I felt a flash of shame... for not having thought about those questions myself. I felt a little deflated. And then the phrase *ideas are not personal* pushed me beyond emotions that were not helping me or the company. I've been here three weeks now and have had countless conversations like the one you just heard. Every time it gets easier — I remember I wouldn't be here if the company did not value my contributions."

Jenny read the tattoo on the inside of Jeff's left forearm: FEAR = Face Everything And Rise.

"Working at SOBS is teaching me to think differently," Jeff continued. "The culture consistently makes it clear that mistakes are fine — welcome even — as long as I keep learning and growing. I am able to focus on my work without interpersonal drama. There's no LOL or IMHO. I'm beginning to understand the difference between fact and opinion... and to recognize it's healthy for opinions to be shared and debated with vigor. Not only do I have projects in process... *I* am a project in process."

Late in the afternoon Jen shut down her computer, stuffed the SOBS welcome packet into her bag, and headed for the exit.

"See you on Monday?" Jeff called.

Jen nodded her agreement and replied, "Enjoy your weekend." There wasn't a speck of doubt in her mind that she wanted to work here. She wouldn't be among the *many*... Jen was certain she had the fortitude to face everything and rise.

On Sunday morning, Jen took the opportunity to give the practice of radical truth a test drive with her sister Amy. The two had a standing brunch date at a quaint Mexican restaurant midway between their apartments. The regular meet-up had been Jen's suggestion and she sometimes felt that Amy was distracted and in a rush to leave — her mood as heavy as the cheese-covered refried beans on their plates.

Jen dialed Amy.

"Hey Jen. What's up? Are we still on for brunch?"

"Yes... unless, ummm... You know you don't *have* to, right? I love seeing you, but I've had a sense that you're keeping our date to be nice — not because you want to. I saw a poster in the break room at SOBS on Friday. It said, *There is no room for BS, unless it's burritos and salsa.* Be honest? I promise I won't break into pieces if you don't want to meet today."

Amy burst into laughter. "Burritos and salsa! That's so great. Yes! I want to see you and hear about your first day at your new job. And then... I'll tell you what's been distracting me on our Sunday date. You're very perceptive Jen. See you in a couple of hours."

Just create; stay curious; be grateful.

———————

22

VENTURE

Pennies roll, the dice is stacked.

– Margaret O'Brien

$\mathcal{N}$an rounded the corner and looked directly into the face of the new day. When she closed her eyes, ten suns glowed behind her lids — five per eye. Their configuration reminded her of a nickel face on a die, only the center dot slid toward the lower left, much like the birthmark on her right thigh.

Over the course of her life, Nan had traced the brown specks countless times with her index finger, repeating patterns without much thought. The discoloration was fading with time. Nan stopped to inspect it, and could no longer see a single brown freckle where five were once so prominent. *Perhaps this was a sign? Has the time come to shift from accepting my fate to pursuing my destiny?*

She tossed a wave to a group of teens waiting at the corner for a morning bus. Staring at the ground, or a phone in their hands, not a single kid looked in her direction. Wanting to shake the world a little, Nan stepped outside of her comfort zone and called, "Good Morning!" A boy she remembered ringing her doorbell to sell fundraiser popcorn, wreaths, and gift wrap looked up and raised his hand to hip level. And, even though the response was about as limp as a day old banana peel, Nan considered the small interaction a triumph for them both.

She looped a cul de sac that was home to dueling dogs. A beagle howled, a doberman woofed, and a chihuahua yip-yapped. Thinking about a conversation she recently overheard while grocery shopping, Nan added her giggle to the choir.

A girl young enough to be carrying a doll, and yet too big to ride in the cart, was complaining of a tummy ache. The child's mother said, "Daddy gave you too much ice cream after lunch!" And the child's father said, "I must not have given you enough ice cream after lunch!" The party of three all started laughing, relieved by the possibility that all questions do not have definite answers.

Nan thought about how, for most of her life, she'd

believed things happened to her — how she'd let other people's lenses define what she was seeing through hers. By golly, if the pundits, PTA president, or her grandfather presented themselves as authorities, Nan was quick to jump on their trains. She'd been accepting her fate, as if she had no personal agency. *How will pursuing my destiny look different?*

Nan was ready to roll her own die.

Pennies roll, the dice is stacked.

———

23

WHISPER

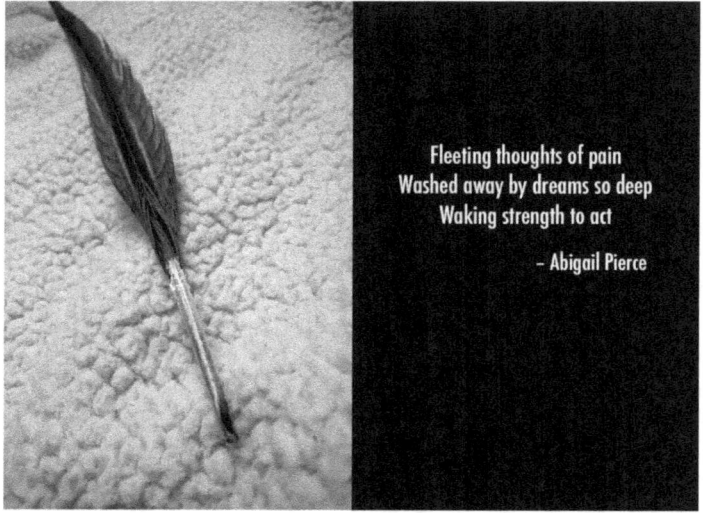

Fleeting thoughts of pain
Washed away by dreams so deep
Waking strength to act

– Abigail Pierce

et's see what happens, Audrey thought while looking at her wrinkled brow in the vanity mirror.

A tension headache snaked its route across her right trapezius, wound itself around her cervical spine, and struck a pounding staccato at the base of her skull. Ignoring the label's directions, she popped three ibuprofen and lay down on her bed. Covering her eyes and forehead with her grandmother's hand-stitched pillowcase, Audrey felt relief — not so much from the pain, but from a welcome sense of invisibility. *If I can't see you, you can't see me.* In her vulnerable state, she resorted to the rationality of a nine-month-old playing peek-a-boo.

Audrey took deep slow breaths, until she fell asleep.

Let's see what happens, Audrey thought when she woke.

Eyes still closed, she took stock. The beat at the base of her skull was gone. Her inquisitive hands explored the muscles around her collar bones, the sides of her neck, and her jaw. With the gentleness of a mother tending a feverish child, Audrey traced her eyebrows and circled her eye sockets. The headache had evaporated — atomized in her dreams.

It took mere moments for her to remember the quills she carried — stuck in places where she couldn't reach. Audrey had built an invisible shell to protect herself from a world that wanted her to be somebody else. When anxious, she felt the stabs of the unstoppable. When angry, she backed the shafts into whoever she felt was threatening her. And, even though she was aware that causing pain for others only increased her own, she couldn't see another way forward.

Out of habit, Audrey crossed her left arm, followed by her right, over her big, confused heart. Even alone in her safest place, Audrey's breathing came in short inhales and exhales, barely reaching the tops of her lungs. Audrey suspected she fired her sharpest daggers at herself.

It's all your fault. Why can't you fix this? Why don't you understand? You are not working hard enough!

She'd been awake less than a minute and already the pounding in her head was back.

Let's see what happens, Audrey thought as she popped three acetaminophen and laid back down on her bed.

With the right side of her body sinking into the mattress, she pulled her knees to her chest. This allowed space for the quills to unfurl while she protected her soft underbelly. Audrey's thoughts circled her emotional cauldron like vultures circling carrion. She'd read that worry changes nothing, steals joy, and keeps us from doing anything of value and yet, she didn't know how to stop.

It was as if her thoughts were balls shot up the chute of a pinball machine at a rapid fire pace. She once heard on a podcast: If people knew what energies flowed from their thoughts, they'd never have another negative thought in their life. Audrey had her doubts about that... *Don't all humans have negative thoughts?* She'd also heard somewhere that humans can't control their thoughts... They can just watch them gallop around the paddock and do their best to stay out of the way. Some said worrisome thoughts could make you sick. Others said positive thinking could make you rich. Then there was this one liner from a Zen master... You are not your thoughts.

If we are not our thoughts... What are we? Audrey wondered.

She felt peppered with falling darkness as if somebody was grinding a spice mill over her entire body. *There are hundreds of ways I am doing life wrong.*

Audrey craved direction, but when offered advice, she listened, nodded, and half-heartedly tried, before quitting when the suggestion felt like wool on her bare skin. *Is seeking advice a sneaky way to avoid taking responsibility for my decisions? No wonder I have a headache.*

Let's see what happens, Audrey thought when she started the game.

As a child, Audrey read a story about a tiger that when feeling anxious, pulled off one of his dark brown stripes and began to write his problems upon it with a parrot's feather. He'd write down what mama and papa said. He'd write down the black panther's whispers that floated on the night breeze. He'd write down what the sleepy old bear said at the river's edge and all of the pick-a-little-talk-a-little cheeps and chirps from those flying above. After he wrote down all the many thoughts swirling in his head, he folded the stripe, popped it in his mouth and began to chew.

Is that what thinking is? Audrey wondered... *Taking all of the many thoughts and making connections? Deciding which ones fit together to make something whole? Or, is thinking something different? What happens when you stop resisting and rearranging? Do thoughts settle like stirred up sand in a glass of water? Can your next step be seen through water that has become clear?*

Like the tiger, Audrey pulled off an imaginary stripe. She wrote down every thought and angle she could think of with a make-believe pinion. Then she folded her problem laden stripe, popped it into her mouth, and began to chew.

Once again, Audrey fell into a dreamless sleep.

When she woke, she gently nodded her head and ran her fingers along her neck and shoulders — no pain.

She had an almost imperceptible tingle in her belly that was whispering what her next step could be... *Trust yourself and embrace the courage that's been inside you all along. You don't need advice. Nobody knows better how to proceed than you. Live your own questions and every little thing is going to be alright.*

Fleeting thoughts of pain
Washed away by dreams so deep
Waking strength to act

———————

24

XANADU

WHEN YOU FIND YOURSELF
SPARE A THOUGHT FOR THE PERSON
WHO SENT YOU TO LOOK

– STUART JAMES

race was a quiet woman who chose a quiet path. The path was clear, with few branches or obstacles. She meandered forward receiving many blessings along the way. She asked for little, and gave when and where she saw an opportunity.

Did Grace have problems?

Well... for starters she was human. She'd once read that only humans have problems. Additionally, she often felt that she was not enough.

"Enough of what?" you ask.

Aha! That was the crux of the problem. Enough of what? Exactly!

Surely, there is a fee required for all I have been given, Grace thought. *Nothing in this world comes without a price.*

Truth be told, Grace welcomed the challenge of giving more of herself to the world, but what danced before her was a great big question mark. *What to give? Where did her talents lie? What skills could she develop that the world needed?*

From all outward appearances, Grace had little to offer. Nobody was actively seeking her services.

Finding no answers on her well-worn and comfortable path, Grace decided she needed to venture into the forest, throwing caution and complacency to the wind.

Haha, that's funny! Grace didn't know how to throw caution to the wind.

And so, Grace began making the tiniest of excursions among the pine, maples, and oaks... always returning to the safety of the path. Each time she returned, she carried new awareness, a desire for more, and a hint of boldness.

Grace was learning that the universe rewards action.

Grace started saying yes, instead of no. She stopped resisting challenges and chose to see opportunities.

"Grace — Oh, Grace," the animals of the forest called. "Will you come and play with us?"

Eyes downcast, Grace watched the effort and dedication of ants building strong, sturdy hills and tunnels. Eyes looking ahead, Grace took in the acrobatic nature of squirrels foraging and preparing for colder days. Looking up,

Grace saw birds revealing that flying high offers a different perspective. And, although her destiny was yet unclear, Grace believed every outing was leading her closer to the answers she sought.

One cloudy and misty day, Grace felt certain that building ant hills was not her destiny. She headed back toward the safety of the path grateful to cross a possibility off of her list.

Is this how she should proceed? Experimenting and tossing aside that which did not fit?

Standing below a mighty oak days later, Grace peered at twinkles of sunlight penetrating a leafy canopy. From above, a bright red flock of cardinals tweeted loudly, "Come, follow us!"

Not wanting to go back to the hum-drum path, Grace set her trepidation next to the oak's sturdy trunk and followed by foot, for she had no wings to make her fly.

Huffing and puffing, trying to keep up, Grace stepped out of the forest into a lush, bright green meadow. Disoriented and confused, she tried to sort out what she saw. Spread about on the verdant ground were tables carved from the trunks of trees — topped with thick panes of glass.

Tables in a meadow?

Each station held a project in process. There were graphite drawings, paintings, tiny houses built of sticks, feathers fashioned into hats, musical scores, and a multitude of other creations. Grace wondered... *Who is creating these beautiful and interesting things?*

Not a single person was in sight.

A lone cardinal led Grace to an empty table on the edge of the meadow. Much to her surprise, she noticed her name etched in delicate script into the glass. Endless vials of colored sand with names like cerulean, magenta, and lemonade were lined up in rows of three along the table's edge.

Well, this was interesting.

Now what?

The cardinal rejoined its flock that got on with its bird follies — soaring, singing, preening and the like.

Without guides, Grace walked the meadow with the care and attention of hummingbirds seeking the finest nectar. Her hungry eyes dipped and sipped. *Where are the artists?*

When she returned to the table bearing her name, Grace remembered learning about mandalas — intricate designs made by monks with sand. Monks might spend days, weeks, possibly years, creating the most beautiful designs, only to sweep them away upon completion. It was an exercise in non-attachment — a reminder that life on earth is not about the destination, but rather the journey.

Grace picked up a vial of beige sand and made a tentative line upon her table's translucent top. Her hand was steady, yet reluctant to be bold. *Can I do this?*

Grace stood back and looked at her imperfect creation. Lines wobbled and mismatched colors mingled where they might have stood better alone. Yet, Grace felt satisfaction in her doing. *One small act is worth more than a bushel full of thoughts?*

As the sun began to set, a bluebird led Grace through the forest and back to the path.

At home, Grace found herself longing for the peace she found in the meadow. She yearned to mix colors and to shape her designs into an expression of herself. If others like her were working on their creations, Grace could not see them. It was as if each artist was hidden behind an invisible wall. Before and after Grace worked on her mandalas, she strolled the meadow and explored. Some projects grabbed her attention, offering inspiration and desire to improve her own work. Other pieces were not her cup of tea and she passed them by offering little more than a glance. She loved the freedom to explore at will, nourishing her heart and soul with generous offerings from others.

This world, within walking distance, was so different from the one she came from.

Grace tended to her life on the quiet path, but began making more and more frequent trips to the meadow. In the beginning, she did not tell anybody on the path about her mandalas or the secret space she spirited off to whenever she could find a moment. The meadow was her private, sacred place.

Grace knew what happened when you told people secret things.

A fish with its mouth closed never gets caught.

Grace was not prepared for the questions... what, when, where, how... and especially why.

She didn't know herself.

One blue-sky morning when Grace approached her happy place, she found notes left upon her chair. The notes were from other creators who worked in the meadow: notes commenting on Grace's mandalas! Some offered praise. Others were notes of shared experience — something in Grace's mandalas caused them to remember, think, or feel. Grace felt energized and exhilarated. To share experiences and ideas with others from paths she hadn't yet traveled sparked feelings of great joy.

Have I found my destiny at long last?

Grace embraced creating in the meadow while enjoying

the new community she'd found. Life, indeed, was good —
until — self-importance reared its head. Grace became
attached to the positive messages she was receiving — the
supportive words were like warm sunshine streaming
through a window on a cold and windy day. But, Grace
suspected there was risk in creating to satisfy the tastes of
others. *Will I find myself looking outside, rather than in? And
what might come of the joy I've found?*

In a quiet corner of Grace's mind, questions popped up
like spring clovers. *Where are you going with this work in the
meadow? Is it serving those back on the path? There are bills to
pay and examples to set. Why do you continue to mess about in
the meadow? Isn't it selfish?*

In a flutter, she became the webmaker and the fly.
Caught.

But, but, but, Grace countered, *something is telling me this
is the right thing to do.*

The notes in the meadow seemed to be hinting at something. Maybe there was a way she could turn her mandalas
into respectable art... to share with those back on her
beloved path. Many messages offered encouragement. "Yes,"
they said. "We see something and think you can do this. We
see you have gumption. Keep going; create mandalas; share;
build your skills. You can do this. Like the animals of the
forest, we will help guide you."

Grace's intuition whispered, *Take one step at a time. Learn,
grow, share, and repeat. Pay little heed to passing clouds of doubt.*
And, even though Grace saw creations she thought much
better than hers in the meadow, she accepted a challenge to
remain only in competition with herself.

Grace had faith in what she could not see.

Try to do everything in the world with a mind that lets go. If you let go a little, you will have a little peace. If you let go a lot, you will have a lot of peace. If you let go completely, you will know complete peace and freedom. Your struggles with the world will have come to an end.

~Achaan Chan

When you find yourself
Spare a thought for the person
Who sent you to look

———————

25

YIELD

God blesses parents
with children —
mirrors.

– Roger Jacobs

*F*ully reclined with lids playing possum, I watched her half-fill the vase. *Did she think I was asleep?* I'd spent a lifetime watching through eyelids at half-staff, appearing disinterested so as to avoid attention while soaking in every detail of my surroundings. An under-cover career taught me to see well below the surface.

Nobody paid me much attention before, but now I was downright invisible. Frail body — frail mind is what they seemed to think.

Not her, though, not Andi — Andi always took time to stop and ask about my day, my grandchildren, or the book I'd been reading. There was no hiding from Andi.

She reached into the drawer, her hand shuffling through the odds and ends of rubbish tossed without care and matted into a mess. *Good girl* — She chose the scissors with the blue handle. I knew from experience that snipper had sharp blades.

Yes... My caretakers occasionally allowed me the joy of trying to cut intricate snowflakes in winter and paper flowers in spring. When you hover somewhere between nine and ten decades of age, you have to get your thrills where you can find them. I reap so much joy recalling escapades of days gone by. Oh, how I loved to create works of art from scraps of paper then — and now.

Well, I knew what Andi was up to and it wasn't paper crafts. She stopped at the patio door and slipped into those strange looking rubber shoes with the holes on top. *Do you know they sell charms to fit in those holes?* Andi's had Snow White, a tulip, and an orange and white striped fish. *What is this world coming to?* Everybody is selling something to somebody.

Andi, always considerate and kind, slid the door open and closed as gently as a new mother swaddling a babe. I rolled in the blessing of her company. The twinge of shame about playing possum while watching her every move was completely erased by, by... a heart so full it could burst.

Through the freshly polished glass, I saw her first stop

was daffodils in shades of freshly churned butter. Their orange centers reminded me of the morning sun's rays on the eastern horizon. I watched as Andi cut two Narcissus that had just started to open. This girl knew what she was doing. Only amateurs cut fully open blossoms.

Next, she walked to the lilac bush, the one with deep purple flowers. She held the daffodils up close and I could see she was pleased with the combination. Snip, snip, snip. Good thing she took the sharp scissors. The woody stems of the lilacs could sometimes be a real bugger to cut through.

And then, she disappeared from view. I guessed at where she went. That lovely bouquet she was assembling needed a touch of green. Andi knew it as well as I did.

Sure enough, when she emerged from the hedge, I could see the lime green of newly sprouting American pussy willow buds. Andi had an eye for color and shape all right. I pondered where such awareness came from.

Back inside, she slipped off her ugly shoes and breezed past my lollygagging legs. I was familiar with the scent of her perfume. It'd been her favorite since she was a teen.

Sleeping old man was the role I played while she trimmed stems and arranged her forager's bounty in an old pickle jar vase. When she approached the oval, cherry wood table in front of my chair, I could no longer keep quiet.

I opened my eyes as wide as zinnia blossoms and asked, "Andi, did you use tepid water? You don't want to shock the poor flowers."

"Daddy! I thought you were asleep. I meant for these to be a surprise. Were you spying on me?"

"Only for your whole life," I replied. "I take my work very seriously... and you are the most important plant I've ever raised."

God blesses parents with children — mirrors.

Childhood wisdom... to
easily make friends.

– Katarina Tajiri

*E*mily's mother watched from her seat on a wrought iron bench as her daughter approached the girls who held a red and blue length of braided rope. She was close enough to see and hear, but far enough to give Emily space to shine.

"Can I play?" Emily asked.

The girl with a blond ponytail smiled and said, "Yes!"

The girl with a brown bob that matched the cartoon character's hair on her shoes frowned.

Emily and her mother had moved into the neighborhood less than a week ago, and both welcomed opportunities to build new friendships.

At the age of six, Emily wore her gentle nature like a pair of monarch wings. Keeping her head tilted down, she raised only her eyes to the frowning girl. Emily smiled and said, "My name is Emily. What's yours?"

"Maggie." Her brown eyes met Emily's blue.

Emily extended her hand and said, "Here, I'll take your end of the rope. You can jump first!"

Childhood wisdom... to easily make friends.

AFTERWORD

Once upon a time, a quiet little mouse hid among the shadows — plain, drab, and colorless. She twitched her whiskers and observed life from a safe distance.

Then one fine spring morning, as a brilliant orange sun rose in a cerulean sky, that quiet little mouse plucked up her courage and dashed into the light where she met turtles, and crickets, and bluebirds — Oh my!

She also met a great big, black, furry, four-leg who assured her that what's small to the dog looms large to the mouse.

"Walk with me?" asked the dog.

And so it began.

My name is Gail.

I was once a trembling mouse — afraid to step into the fullness of the meadow we call life. Then I picked up a challenge to write and publish one hundred vulnerable words per day. As days stretched into months and years and hundreds of words turned into pages, I delighted in sharing the lessons of my life.

I offer my lessons to you — stories shared from one friend to another.

The gradual shift from black and white to full color in the landscape on the trilogy's covers reflects my growth as a person and a writer. My hope is that sharing my experiences will inspire you to explore your own colors.

"Walk with me?"

ACKNOWLEDGMENTS

Please write your name here _____.

Thank you for being part of my life and for engaging with my work. I'm a writer who longs for readers... Our connection fuels my joy.

There is a clear line of benevolent provocations between *No Book Gail* and *Wandering Words, Meandering Muses,* and *Flourishing Fictions.*

Seth Godin — Thank you for the Akimbo platform where my confidence had space to grow. The Creative's Workshop connected me to...

Peter Williams — Thank you for a *Productive Accident* leading me to...

Chris Palmore — I'm so very grateful that you invited me to contribute to *Dear Gratitude* and *Dear 2020* — curated story collections of gratitude and hope. Thank you also for introducing me to...

Noosha Ravaghi — You cultivated my confidence with an empowering balance of soft and firm... and like all great leaders, you pushed me out of the nest when I was ready to fly. Thank you.

Gary Breads — You made a beautiful bridge to...

Kara Masters — You are a mighty fine book doula. I am hopeful we will birth many more works together.

ABOUT THE AUTHOR

Gail Boenning wonders, wanders, and writes.

More than anything... She wants YOU to go where your mind is challenged, your heart beats with excitement, and your essence hears the voice of Possibility.

ALSO BY GAIL BOENNING

Wandering Words: A Walk from A to Z

Meandering Muses: Inspirations from A to Z